I AM SHADE

MAYANK SINHA

AF516834

BlueRose Publishers

First Published in December 2019

ISBN: 978-93-5347-936-7

BLUEROSE PUBLISHERS

www.bluerosepublishers.com

info@bluerosepublishers.com

+91 8882 898 898

Cover Design:

Tyngshain Pariat

Typographic Design:

Tanya Raj Upadhyay

Distributed by: BlueRose, Amazon, Flipkart, Shopclues

I AM SHADE

Dedicated

To all my mentors who always had faith in me.

Contents

01

After a tiring day at work, I headed back to my apartment, to my only companion who was eagerly waiting for me. As soon as I opened the door to my apartment, it embraced me with a cold gust of wind. By now I had become used to it–generally referred to by others as–silence. I locked the door behind my back and after taking my shoes off, strolled straight to my bed. I plopped on my bed with a sigh. *Does everyone have a destiny? Do people like me find someone who can love them? Will I ever be able to do something better with my life?* Question after question flooded my mind. All of a sudden, the doorbell rang, thereby, pulling me out of my trance.

I slowly dragged myself across my apartment and opened the door. A teenage boy stood before me. He was wearing an oversized jacket that had a logo on its pocket which said Vd's pizza. "Are you Jayden Smith?", he asked in an unsure voice. "Yes, I am", I replied.

"Here is your cheese burst pizza—with extra onion and without tomatoes", he said and handed over the pizza-box to me. I took it from him, and he left. I balanced the hot box to my dining table and started to open it. I pulled a slice and took my first bite, being careful not to drop cheese all over the table. The receipt at the table caught my eye. I kept my slice in the box and picked up the receipt:

Name: Jayden Smith, Order date: 22-Oct-2018, Order time: 21:40, Location: Sacramento, CA.

Even though I had paid for the order online, I was just cross-checking if everything in the receipt was all right. After confirming it, I continued to devour my pizza, peacefully.

After the meal, I changed into my pajamas and went to bed. *So—Mr Jayden Smith—another day ended in your twenty-two years of existence!* I thought to myself. *The guy who worked in FedEx. Is this, then, going to be my story when I die?* Consumed by such deep thoughts, my eyelids started getting heavy and I was slowly engulfed into darkness...

[BEEP! BEEP! BEEP!]

The sound woke me up. Still sleepy, I looked at the time: 7:00 AM. Okay, five more minutes, I thought and closed my eyes. Suddenly, I woke up with a start, glanced at the clock: 8:45 AM. *Shit! Shit! Shit—not again!* I jump-started my day by skipping bath, breakfast and a proper dressing sense. I Reached work. The day went by. As I was walking home, I remembered that I had to buy detergent soap. So, I took a shortcut from the lane near my office. It is a narrow lane where darkness seems to constantly battle for total control over the place, with only a small flickering yellowish, dim light coming from some lamp in the only shop present in the lane. By the looks of it, it seemed like a Chinese antique shop, but I had never entered it. Perhaps because I didn't think the shop would have anything of my interest.

Today, however, it was different while I was passing by the shop. A silver gleam caught my attention. I stopped in order to have a better look. On a quick inspection through the window, I could see a silver Dragon statue, kept in a glass case at the farthest end of the shop. The lamplight on being reflected from the surface of the statue was making the dragon look alive, with its scales appearing to be in constant motion. *This looks cool, let me have a closer look*, I thought to myself and entered the shop. As I opened the door, a damp and old smell greeted me as my host. It was a small shop, with two glass cupboards on both sides, and a reception desk in between. The items and showpieces were placed on the shelves of these cupboards. The dragon statue that I came for, was kept in the far end of the second row of the left cupboard. Since I could see no one in the shop, I walked up to the statue. I thought that maybe if I wait for some time, somebody might show up, because calling out to someone aloud or shouting somehow didn't seem appropriate at that moment. I was now examining the statue and estimating its price.

"Do you like it?" A slow paced and shrill voice questioned me. It startled me for a second, and then I turned. I could see a small, old Chinese woman standing behind the counter. She was wearing a pale-coloured cloth which looked somewhat like a robe. Her hair, silver in colour, was carefully tied in a bun and her face was wrinkled. The different ridges and curves on her face seemed like the Alps' range of life experiences with her black eyes seated in one of the curves of the mountain range.

"Yes, it looks kinda nice," I replied.

"It is a rare statue, and I myself brought it from my ancestral hometown in China". "Yeah, right. And I am the next Chinese emperor in disguise," I thought to myself with a smirk. "Okay ... nice. So, how much would it cost?" I asked.

"It's $7 but you seem like a nice boy with a good taste, so, I will give it to you for $5."

There's no way I am going to pay $5 for that thing, I decided. "It's too costly! I'm sorry but I don't think I will be able to buy it," I said and gestured to leave the shop.

"Okay, wait, wait dear child. Don't you go! Final price for you will be $3—only for you," she declared.

"Fine," I replied. It seems like a decent price, I thought. "I'll take it." I added and then bought the item, and after running the errand in the market, I came back home.

As soon as I reached home, I hurriedly opened the packaging of the statue, revealing it, and now I could see it in its full glory! On a closer look, I could make out that the dragon was holding a translucent orb in its mouth, and the eyes of the dragon were made out of a gem of red colour. The stand of the statue had something engraved on it, it was written :

死亡帶來生命

On putting it on google image search, it roughly came out to be a phrase that said:

Death Brings Life

At first, it seemed odd to me. But since it was giving me a full anime vibe, I decided to ignore the other thoughts for the time being and was observing closely each of the statue's details. After getting satisfied with my research, I placed the statue on my bedside table. I was very happy with my purchase. It looked really fancy at my bedside table. So, after getting ready for bed, I turned off the lights and while looking at the statue which was reflecting the night light, my eyes drooped heavily and it all became dark soon.

02

[BEEP ... BEEP ... BEEP ... BEEP!]

A constant sound was echoing in my ears. As I slowly tried to open my eyes, a flood of white light entered it and caused me to close them. After a few seconds, I tried again, but this time more cautiously. As my eyes adjusted to the surrounding light, I could make out a white colour ceiling, and then I slowly moved my eyes to the left. I could see a stainless-steel table with a flower pot on top. There was a small clock beside it as well; it read 8:00. It must be daytime, I thought to myself. Turning my eyes to other side, I could see an empty bed with a white bed sheet. It took me a second before all the sirens in my head went off.

I woke up with a start. I had a quick glance at my surroundings. I slowly realized ... I was in a hospital. *Wait! What?! A Hospital! What the hell am I doing in a Hospital?* A wave of questions started to drown me. Since I saw no one around, I pressed the buzzer for help. But I couldn't hear even a distant echo of the bell. I tried calling out loud, "Hello? Is anyone there?" But no reply came from anywhere. It freaked me out even more.

I decided to get out and look for someone myself. I removed the bedsheet that was covering me and started to get out of my bed.

[THUD!]

The sound echoed through the room as I fell on the floor. A chill ran down my spine as I gradually registered that I was unable to feel my legs. My heart was racing, and my throat had become dry. I was sweating profusely. I tried to get up, but it was in vain. So, I tried to drag myself to the door. A nervous chill ran down my spine, I was panicking, as my arms got a grip of the ground and pulled my body towards the door. My ears were ringing, and my mind had gotten completely blank.

I couldn't figure out what was going on. *Why the hell was I in a hospital? And above all–why was I unable to feel my legs? What was happening to me?* As I was about to reach the door, I could hear footsteps approaching. I yelled, "Hey, help me please!" The footsteps had now become faster and then the door opened.

From where I was, I could make out four pairs of legs–three male and one female. "Oh no! What happened in here?", the female enquired. But before I was able to reply, I could feel three men trying to get a hold on me in order to pick me up. I didn't resist. After they helped me get back on my bed, I ranted, "I was trying to get out, but couldn't feel my legs, and I fell, but first tell me, where am I? A-and how did I get here? And who are you? What the hell is happening?"

I could see the lady now. She was wearing a doctor-jacket over a green uniform. Her eyes—beneath a pair of cat-eye glasses—were black, and so was her hair, giving her face a look of innocence which was highlighted by her porcelain skin. She looked almost my age or maybe a year or two older.

She stood in front of my bed and seemed a bit overwhelmed by my questions. So, she took a moment to flip through the file she had with her and then answered.

"I understand that you must be having a lot of questions, but don't worry, it is normal for people waking up from a coma to have such thoughts. And you said you couldn't feel your legs; I suspect it to be paresthesia. Or in general terms, it can be said that your legs are still asleep."

Coma was the last thing that I heard, and after that I was unable to jump back to reality. I was so dumbstruck by her answers, that I fell short of words. "For how long have I been here?", I questioned after trying to get a hold on my thoughts.

"It has been two years since the blast ... the time when you were brought at our facility."

"The what–?", I fumbled quizzically while speaking.

"Yes; oh wait! you must be unaware—-a bomb blast had taken place in your locality, Mr Smith. It had wiped out your entire city. Thousands had died that fateful night. The rescue team somehow managed to dig out your body from the debris of your apartment. It was clearly a miracle that you had survived. Your condition was very critical when you were brought in here. We didn't think you would be able to make it. But somehow you hung on," she finished.

"B-but ... what about my family ... I mean, my mom? Where is she now? She lives on 9th Avenue. How is she?" I asked, panic-stricken. "Sorry to say, your mother is no more. She had had a heart attack. Back then, you were already declared dead by the authorities, and this news hit your mother too hard. When the rescue team finally found your body, our team tried to reach her. But from what I can see in your contact history report it seems it was too late until then" she replied. Tears were rolling down my cheeks and I wiped them off quickly. "Really sorry about your loss," she consoled. I was feeling very angry, outrageous and helpless–all at the same moment. I just wished I had visited her once! "Just leave me alone," I blurted harshly. I didn't mean to, but it just came out like that. She didn't say a word and quietly left the room.

After she left, my grief knew no bounds. I sobbed uncontrollably. I buried my face in my pillow so that no one could hear me cry, and then I just cried my heart out until I fell asleep.

The monotonous beep of the machine woke me up the next morning. I was still drowsy but I decided to sit up. So many things had happened in my life in these past days. I did not know what to do or think or feel. These tragedies were so horrific that it seemed that my mind had somewhat slipped into denial in order to protect me from going insane and breaking apart, and in this process, turned my heart into stone. I was living a nightmare.

The lady doctor had advised me some acupuncture tricks that I could use to bring senses back to my legs, and I had been doing them. I cannot say that the result was immediate and useful, but now at least I had some sort sensation even though I was still unable to move them entirely.

03

Three weeks had passed since I had woken up. I had gained control over my feet and was finally able to walk slowly. The doctor said that in a few more weeks I will be able to get back to normalcy. Until now I only tried to walk in the hospital premises; there was even a training room downstairs. Today, as I was being discharged, I decided to go outside to visit my locality. The hospital staff was very helpful. They had already arranged my stuff, so I got ready and moved out. As I got my belongings, I could only find a tattered nightdress that I was wearing that night. I slowly made my way out of the hospital and decided to take a cab to my old place. Across the street there was a cab stand, I waited for some time and got myself a ride to my place.

After a fifteen-minutes' drive, the driver halted in a barren area. "We have arrived", he said. I gave him a blank expression, as the place seemed to be in the middle of nowhere. Then I had a look in the GPS screen fixed at his dashboard and saw that our location was correct. A little confused, I handed him out the money and got out of the car. As I walked, what I saw left me shocked.

It seemed as if I was standing in front of a sea of black debris. It seemed that the area had been levelled by an enormous force. For as far as I can see, there were only debris and rubble in each direction. *Jesus! What the hell happened over here?* Trying to find any living creature–humans in particular–I started scanning the area. Just then, something caught my eye. From where I was standing, there was someone at a distance opposite me, bent onto the ground as if trying to find something. The figure of the person was not clear, but I could make out that he was wearing some kind of black hoodie. At first I thought that it must be some homeless guy on a scavenger hunt. But, as he was removing the rubble, there was something off about his movements. Now, under normal circumstances, I would have just left and not bothered him. But since now I was in the middle of nowhere and as they say, that curiosity killed the cat. I decided to approach him. Only God knows why.

As I slowly started to move towards him, I was trying to place my steps carefully as I did not want to spook him out. There was a clink! I stopped where I was, and looked down to see that I had stepped on a piece of glass. I carefully removed my foot from it, trying not to make any other sound. But as I looked up, I realized that it was already too late. The guy had heard the sound and had stood up. His back was facing me, what I thought to be a hoodie was actually a robe that seemed to cover his whole body, the most iconic thing about the robe was that it had a white marking on it which looked like a cat's head from where I was standing. "Hey! Wait–I mean no harm," I said in a louder voice. He waited for a moment and then made a run. "What the...!!" I exhaled, while hurriedly straightening my stance, and getting ready to go after him. My legs were not supporting me enough. I was hurriedly limping towards him, while shouting at him, "Hey wait! I just need to talk." Suddenly, I hit something on the ground. Shit! Shit! Oww! [THUD!] I fell face forward in the rubble.

Oh man! Damn it! I cursed under my breath. I picked myself up, brushed my face and wiped my eyes clean in order to clear my vision. While dusting my clothes, I looked in the direction of the guy, but couldn't see anything. He must've gotten away, I finally conjectured. As I stood up, I looked down upon the thing that had made me fall. It looked like some kind of mound in the ground covered in dust. I decided to take a closer look. As I sat down to inspect it, it felt like some strong object oval in shape. As I plucked it out from the rubble, I could see the dust falling from it, revealing its true shape. I wiped it with my hands and kept staring at the object. I was both amazed and shocked to see that it was the Dragon Statue. The same one that I had bought *that* night.

While returning to my allocated room, a question that lingered in my mind was that, *If the blast was so huge and terrific, then how the hell did I manage to survive it?* I couldn't think of a logical explanation. Since I was recovering at a decent pace now, I was shifted to a room in a building complex next to the hospital. It was a service apartment which was now being used to house the people affected by the blast. I cleaned the statue as I got back, and after having my dinner, I went back to my room to sleep. As I laid on my bed, I kept wondering about the guy in the hoodie and what could be the possible reason for him to react in such a manner. I must have startled him, I guessed.

As the days were passing, my life seemed to have become a question mark in itself. I did not know if I still had a job or not; neither did I know for how long would I be able to survive like this on my savings. I had already lost the most important people from my life. All I had left of them were memories and now I felt completely helpless and had no clue from where to start my life again. All these thoughts pooled in my head, and a tear trickled down my cheek, as I fell asleep.

Loud noises echoed into my room from outside, waking me up from my slumber. I checked the clock; it was still 2 AM. The sounds were muffled but it seemed like people were arguing about something. Still yawning and rubbing my eyes, I decided to check it out myself. As I opened the door, I could now clearly hear the words. The voice seemed of a man, shouting "Where is he? Let us know and nobody gets hurt." A woman answered while sobbing, "I have already told you, I do not know him. I cannot help you, just let me go." As my eyes adjusted to the brightness of the corridor, I could see two men in black suits. They were both well-built and were wearing black sunglasses. *Queer*, I thought. One of them was holding the woman by her hair and the other stood there as if looking out for his partner. They both were holding a gun in their hand and looked like henchmen. The other patients had also come out on hearing the commotion but were afraid to utter a word or disrupt the ongoing situation. They looked at the woman with pity and horror-stricken faces. As I stepped out of my room, the creak from my door echoed in the whole corridor.

The other guy's attention was drawn towards me. He studied me for a second and then nudged his partner who was questioning the lady. He too looked up and saw me, then, in a second, loosened his grip on the lady. They slowly started to walk–towards me. I stood there stunned and perplexed, as I was unable to understand why these strangers were coming towards me. In a matter of seconds, I was facing two huge men. These two towered in front of me. At first, they did not say anything but simply stood there as if confirming my identity. "Yes? Can I help you?" I finally mustered the courage to speak. "Are you Jayden Smith?", asked one of them. "Yes I am, who are you?", I countered. They looked at each other, and then one of them said, "It doesn't matter." Before I could react to it, they forcibly covered my mouth with their hand and pressed the gun against my chest.

[SHOOK! CLUNK! SHOOK! CLUNK!]

All I could hear were these metallic noises. After this, a streak of pain seared through my chest. This pain was unbearable and slowly I couldn't control my body. My chest was leaking some liquid which was trickling down my clothes, and slowly, breathing was becoming more and more difficult. These two men stood with stern faces in front of me, as I collapsed on the ground. Now this liquid from my chest was flooding the floor. It reached my face and while lying on the ground, I realized that it was my own blood that I was soaked in. It was gradually becoming a tremendous effort to even keep my eyelids open. I was trying my level best to remain conscious. I saw the two men slowly walk away from me, as I could hear their footsteps fading away. It felt as if an elephant was standing on top of me, with my body collapsing under its weight. It felt as if my time had come. There was complete darkness, and the whole world seemed to be covered in a curtain of silence, my old friend. And now it felt as if I was ready to become a part of this silence.

04

I could see a streak of light at some distance. I decided to go towards it. As I was reaching closer, it started to get brighter and brighter until I was surrounded by white light. Finally, I was able to open my eyes. As my eyes adjusted to the brightness, I realized that I was lying on dry grass, and I was in some sort of cave. After a moment of self-realization, the memories of the tragedy that had befallen me came rushing back to me. My breathing became frantic, and I started looking at the surroundings in order to make sure that those two men weren't around. And I was glad to confirm that they weren't. I was breathing heavily and it took me a moment to calm down. But as I did, I lifted my right hand to wipe my sweaty face. Or rather, what I thought to be my sweaty face. As I touched my face, I felt gluey mass covering a portion of it. I decided to wipe it off. As I caught the gluey stuff, it suddenly started to move. I freaked out and I threw it away immediately. *Yuck!* A chill ran down my spine as I saw it was—an earthworm. As I threw the worm away, I noticed something strange. I noticed that my hand felt different than before. It felt as if my hand was covered in some kind of rug. Closely examining it, I couldn't believe my eyes. They were actually feathers. *What!* I bellowed. I quickly looked upon my body and saw that it was also covered in the same feather. Horrified, I reached to feel my face, and my eyes seemed smaller, but when I tried to touch my mouth and nose, it seemed as if they had been combined into some kind of conical structure. It took me some time to realize that I might have become some kind of human-bird hybrid. *That's completely absurd! Am I hallucinating?* I searched for explanations. *This has to be a dream of some kind, it'll be over soon, right?*

I stood up and slapped myself, hoping against hope to end this nightmare, but it only confirmed that I was fully awake. Now as I tried to walk out of the cave, I realized that something was moving with me and it strangely felt a part of me. *Yeah, why not!* It was my goddamn tail! I now had a tail!

As I somehow managed to reach the opening of the cave, or what I thought to be a cave, a fresh breeze welcomed me with a similar scent of the morning breeze. And it was now, that it started to sink in that I was not part-human, part-bird, rather, I had metamorphosed into a complete bird on a nest in the bark of a tree. As I stood on the edge of the nest, I could see the green grass and the clear blue sky. But for some reason, there was too much noise over there. It seemed as if 100 people had decided to greet each other all at once. On looking to the branches left to me, I could see many different birds sitting on it. But the strange thing was that I could understand what they were saying. *Whaaaaat! All this ... this cannot be true!* The first reaction was shock.

"Hey, you look new here," I suddenly heard a voice from my immediate right. The voice was a little deep, but it startled me, and as I turned to see who it was, I lost balance and fell from the tree. In a matter of split seconds, I was accelerating towards the ground with great speed. My mind blanked out as I couldn't bring myself to think of anything. So, out of fear, I closed my eyes. But after a while, the wind kept gushing in and kept touching my body. *By now I should be on the ground, right?* I was utterly confused. The wind kept gushing past me, now it seemed that I was gaining a constant speed. I slowly opened my eyes. At first, I could see a green flare passing below me. Then as my vision cleared, I could see that it was the grass that was passing by quickly as I was gliding over it. Now I saw that by instinct I had opened my arms or wings in this case. After a few more moments, I learnt that I could even steer my wings in different directions in order to control my speed accordingly and even increase or decrease my altitude while flying. *This is so Cool!* I screamed with joy.

As I was gliding, I heard the same voice again calling to me and saying, "Hey wait up, I am sorry I didn't mean to surprise you, sorry!" I turned back my head slightly to the left and then I could see that it was a green colored parrot that was approaching me from behind. He quickly flapped his wings and was now flying parallel to me. He looked at me and said, "Hi, I am Sicco." I nodded in acknowledgement. "Sorry about that," he added. At this moment I had become so confused that I had stopped thinking. One moment I was a normal guy living a normal life, then the next moment I was a bird talking to another bird. Now, instead of freaking out, I decided not to do anything and just go with the flow, because my logical reasoning clearly had come to a halt.

"Hey, follow me. Let's get to some height, this area is not safe for us," Sicco informed. I followed him and then we perched on the branch of an old tree. From here the view was clear–I was in a park, which was surrounded by a concrete jungle. As far as I could see now, the boundary of the park was square and was fenced with a brick wall, with each side having an entrance gate.

"So where are you from?" Sicco asked. "Earth," I replied sarcastically.

"Earth? never heard of that, is it outside the pisco?" he enquired.

"Pisco?" I asked, dumbfounded.

"Yes, outside the pisco," he replied while pointing to the park's fence.

"Oh! You mean the park ..." I replied, a little relieved.

"Park?" he questioned again, looking confused.

"Never mind. it's okay. Well, yes, Earth is outside 'pisco'," I quickly replied in order to avoid any further confusion.

"Okay, but till you are here, let me tell one very important thing," he said.

"Alright ... and what is that?" I asked.

"Stay away from the kiskos," he answered firmly.

"Kiskos?" I was bewildered.

"Yes, yes kiskos," he replied while pointing to a man walking in the park.

"Okay..." *So, this is how birds see us–I mean ... humans...*

"See, not all of them are bad. Some of them even bring us food to eat, but most of them will try to hurt you," he informed with a hardened face.

"And since you don't know who is who, 'tis better you stay away from them," he added.

I simply replied with a nod.

While I was sitting, something caught my eye near the park's fence. I looked closely and saw that it looked like a small person, who was dressed in a robe exactly like the one I saw before. He was walking close to the fence on the outer side of the park. He was walking as if he was in a hurry to get somewhere. This time I decided not to let him get away, and maybe if I try to reach him, I might get to know what has happened to me.

“Okay Sicco, it was really nice meeting you. Now I have somewhere to go,” I told him.

“Okay, do come and meet me when you’re around next time,” he replied and flew away.

I now flew to the boundary wall and sat on top of it, scanning for that guy. I spotted him. He was turning towards a lane on the street. I quickly flew, following him. But as soon as I reached the entrance of the lane, I was surprised to see that the lane was a dead end, and there was no sign of the guy. From my size, that lane seemed to be like an enormous stretch of land, with a huge wall at the end. As I got closer to the wall, I suddenly sensed something move behind me. I quickly turned around. My heart was racing, I had become conscious of my surroundings. But nothing, there was nothing to see. It was an empty lane from where I came in. SWISH! A rustling sound echoed. I turned around once again, to check if there was something wrong with the wall. Still nothing. But as soon as I turned towards the wall, I realized that I had looked in every direction except for one–upwards.

I slowly turned my head to see what was above me. I was left terrified by what I saw. The hooded guy was hovering above me. I couldn’t make out his face in the hood. All I could see were a pair of gleaming blue eyes that were monitoring every move of mine. As soon as my eyes met his, the look told me that it was too late for me. I instantly looked away and tried to fly. But it was as if I was being held back by some power. And in a fraction of a second, I was covered in darkness. I tried to move and scream but it all seemed pointless.

05

A streak of white light was visible now. It seemed comforting. I started to move towards it. The closer I got to it, the larger the ball of light appeared. I walked until I was ultimately surrounded by white light. It was so bright that I was unable to see anything, and then I opened my eyes.

As my vision cleared, I could see that I was in a dingy room. In front of me, there were three people sitting. All of them were wearing some kind of orange-hued clothes. My head was too heavy, for I couldn't think straight. I was in a chair, and on each side of me stood the hooded guys. I wanted to run away from the place but it felt impossible. I felt powerless at that moment. However, something brought me huge relief as my body felt normal now. Even though I was unable to lift my fingers, it just felt good to realize that now I had them. My limbs still felt numb. As I sat on the chair, I saw a hooded person coming towards me, with a cup. As he brought it closer to my lips, I could make out that it was a dark brown liquid, with a strong but sweet smell. I was in no state to resist drinking it. The person just held my head in a firm grip and made me gulp the liquid down. The liquid tasted a little funny–it was warm and I could feel the warmth travel my body as the liquid made its way down my throat. It made me feel better, and gradually the dizziness went away. It took me a while but now I was back to my senses. I adjusted my posture and sat properly on the chair. Feeling much better, I consciously looked at the men sitting in front. I could now make out that the three people in front of me were some kind of old monks. Each of them was bald and had a white beard, and it was really difficult to differentiate one from another. However, the person at the center looked distinguished, as his clothes had a slightly darker shade than the others and he was sitting on an elevated platform higher than the others. I guessed maybe he was their leader.

"Welcome, Mr Smith, I am Sheng." the old person on the left said in a low voice.

"How do you know my name?" I asked, surprised.

"We know much more than your name, Mr Smith," he replied with a smile.

I was confused with his reply, but I continued to ask, "What is this place? Where am I now? What is happening to me?" My mind seemed to now explode full of questions.

"This place is known as the Sanctum," he answered calmly. "I can understand that you might be having a lot of questions, I promise that they all will be answered as and when the time comes. But first you must rest," he said, while signaling the hooded man who was standing behind me.

Overpowered by both mental and physical exhaustion, even I thought that it was a better idea to take some rest first at that moment. The people escorted me to a room. The corridor through which I was taken seemed like a castle from an old Chinese movie. My room was third to the left, from where I came. This room was smaller than the previous room. Where I was made to sit with the monks.It had a mattress laid on the floor on one end, and a sliding-door cupboard on the other. I slid the door close behind me. There were too many things on my mind right now–

First, what was I doing here, and what is this place? Second, what was that whole being a bird scenario? Third, Why the hell did I agree to these people in one go?

These three questions were continuously swirling in my head and were making me restless. So, I decided to investigate on my own. I just couldn't wait until that old guy became ready to give me answers.

I slowly opened the door of my room. The corridor was deserted and so I decided to take a walk. I started walking towards the left of my room. I could see there were some similar rooms beside mine but when I tried to open them, they were locked. So, I kept going straight in the same direction until I reached a two-way crossing. One way from it went to the left and the other to the right. I took the left one. I walked straight and then after a few steps, it felt that I have been here before. I opened a door to my left. It was my room. *WHAT! Wait, I think I must've taken some wrong turn somewhere, and since I am new to the place, I must have been lost.* Thoughtfully, I again took the same path, but this time I took the right turn. Once again, after walking a few steps, I was standing in front of my room. *Woah!* I was totally confused and freaking out by now. Where on Earth was this place?!

"Going somewhere, Mr Smith?" I heard a familiar voice coming from behind me. I turned to see that Mr. Sheng was standing in the corridor.

"Oh yeah, actually I was searching for the washroom," I replied hurriedly.

"It is attached with your room, I believe," he said with a smile on his face.

"Oh ok, my mistake, I guess I'll go back in then," I said and then rushed back into my room.

That was a close one! I had mistaken the door to the washroom for the cupboard door that I had seen earlier. I now realized that it was better for me to take rest now. So, I just slipped into my bed and quickly fell asleep.

06

I was woken up by a tap on the wooden frame of my door. Someone was knocking. In a drowsy state, I got out my bed and opened the door. There was a guy in a hood standing in front of me. He looked jolly and was smiling. He was holding a grey cloth folded up in his arms. "Master Sheng has requested your presence in the garden, kindly get changed quickly. Then I will take you to him," he said while handing me the cloth. I noticed that it was a robe just like the one he was wearing. I then got changed and followed him to the master. Surprisingly, now when I took the right turn at the two-way crossing, I ended up in a garden. The garden was really beautiful! It had a small pond on one side of it, and a giant magnolia tree at the center. The master was standing right beneath it and was looking up at the tree. I slowly walked towards him.I could now see him clearly.

He was wearing a orange colour robe. He was bald and had a small black mole on his right cheek. His face had this strange glow, It looked as if his face was constantly radiating good aura from it. He was clean shaven. He looked like he was in his 60's but he had a childlike spark and curiousity in his eyes.

"Hello, Mr Smith! How do you do today?" he greeted me with a warm smile.

"I am fine, thank you," I replied.

"So, as promised, I'll now answer your questions. You may ask whatever you want to know or understand," he said.

"Where am I? What is this place?" I blurted immediately.

"This place is known as the Sanctum, and currently you at the center of it," he replied coolly.

"Okay ... But I meant to ask what does this place stand for, and where exactly is it?" I explained.

"This is a place for lost souls like you; a place in a space in between spaces," he said.

"Wh-what do you mean?" I quizzically stared at him.

"This, I am afraid, you will have to find out for yourself," he replied.

"Ahh! I see ... but why am I here?" I enquired.

"Because you were chosen by the soul-keeper"

"By the who?"

"Oh yes, the soul-keeper. It can take many forms and has no form of its own. You must have seen it somewhere," he answered.

"Ahhh! I am really sorry to say but I have no clue as to what you are saying," I replied, a bit confused.

"Oh yes, forgive me, my child; but you must have come across any of its mortal forms. Have you, at any point, owned any bracelet or any object that you came across accidentally but it felt like it was okay to own it?" he questioned.

I thought for a moment, and then I replied, "I actually recently had bought a dragon statue, because it seemed really cool to own one."

"Could you describe this statue for me?"

"Oh yeah, sure! It was a small statue of a silver-scaled dragon with red eyes, and it had a translucent orb in its mouth"

"*Death Brings Life*," he said.

"Hey wait a minute–how did you know that this was engraved at the bottom of the statue?" I asked, astonished by his words.

"Hmm, it is then confirmed it was indeed the soul-keeper"

"But how can you be so sure? I mean, it was just a statue that I had bought"

"*Death Brings Life* is the message of the soul-keeper, and only the one he chooses can see it, and the fact that you were drawn to this statue knowingly or unknowingly states that it was the soul-keeper, or else how do you think you ended up directly in the sanctum?" he reasoned.

This got me thinking for a while.

"But where is this Sanctum we are in? I mean is it in China or some other side of the world?" I asked.

"Hmm, I'll let you know, but first tell me what do you remember before coming here?" he asked.

"Ah, let me explain ... at first, I was in a hospital, and then I got shot I guess, by some guys, and then ...umm ... I-I remember that when I woke up, I was–a bird! I think it was a dream but it felt so real and–"

"Wait right there, you say that you remember being a bird?" he interrupted.

"Yes, I do. And I also remember that I was chasing this hooded guy, but what happened after that it's hard to recall," I said.

"Hmm ... I see," he said in a serious tone and delved deep into his thoughts.

After a while, he said, "Follow me, I think that you are worthy enough to know this."

I followed him as he took me around the magnolia tree. There was a bench on which he sat and signaled me to sit next to him. I followed his instruction.

"Listen to what I am about to tell you carefully. And this should strictly be only between you and me, as I trust that you are worthy of this knowledge and will keep it safe. So, are you ready Mr Smith?", he looked intently at me, expecting an answer.

I nodded in agreement for a reply.

"Okay. First tell me what understanding do you have of a mortal or I must say a human's life and death?" he asked.

"Err ... I am not an expert at this but from what I have heard or have been taught, once we are born, we have to live our lives. Based on our good or bad deeds during this lifetime, on our death our soul is then sent to the heaven or hell accordingly," I replied hesitatingly.

"Hmm OK," he then went on to ask, "and this soul you say—what do you think it is?"

"As far as I can say, it seems to me that it is some kind of life source for the body and that it keeps us going on in our life and ... well ... I have also been taught that it is immortal." I replied.

"Okay, now tell me, what do you know about time?", he asked.

"Time, ah! I can say that it ... is like ... constantly passing ... I guess; and we live through time from our birth till our death," I replied, fishing for better words.

"Hmm OK," he said.

"See, what I am about to tell you will clear all your doubts, but this knowledge can be overwhelming. So, are you willing to take the risk?" he questioned in a serious tone.

"Yes, I am"

"Alright then, Mr Smith, listen carefully to what I am about to say"

"I hear you"

"My child, there are many ways to explain this but I will try to explain in the simplest way possible. The truth about life and death is that it only exists in the mortal realm. Or as you prefer to call home–or–where mortals live. Actually, the thing you people refer to as the soul is not an energy source or some mystic power that wanders after your body dies. Rather, it is an entity. There is a misconception in mortals that the mind has the consciousness, but to be correct, the mind only represents the conscious part of the soul. The soul is actually an entity, a self-sufficient, self-reliant entity that is beyond time and space. What you mortals call as the body is actually only a temporary vessel for that soul. Which it conjures for the mortal world. All consciousness of every living being lives on a higher plane than you can comprehend. The part you call as the personality of each individual or the behavior pattern of an individual is only one manifestation of that entity. The life you have lived until now, and all your friends and family live, is actually a *test*. A test that each entity has to give in order to be proven that it belongs in the higher plane or—as we call it—in the Realm..." he trailed off.

"So, you mean to say that we are not what we think we are? Like our soul is not what we have been believing until now?" I interrupted.

"Yes, you can better understand it if I give you an example. You must have seen a puppet show where the puppet does what the puppet-master directs him to do. Now, if we assume that this puppet is alive and has, since his birth, lived in this state, from this puppet's point of view, all his actions are his own and whatever he wants to do, he can do. But we know that it's not true, it is only the puppet-master that is in control. Similar to it is the case with mortals when an entity conjures a body, to enter the test, and interact with other entities. The entity gives a part of it in the shell known as the body and then directs it through the test. Just how a puppet-master directs its puppets. And it means that those bodies that you have in your mortal realm are only shells tied by an entity that is beyond your comprehension, and you are always being controlled from a higher dimension. But if you see from a mortal's point of view, then it seems to him that he can do whatever he wants, and whenever he wants. And this, my child, is known as the illusion of choice," he finished.

"Okay, I get that, but how do you explain heaven, hell and other things that we have been taught until now?" I further probed.

"See, every exam has a syllabus," he said with a smile. "And as far as the heaven and hell are concerned, the heaven can be considered the higher plane where all consciousness resides, and hell is where you are actually living your entire life, or if you fail in the test, you will have to be born again and give the same test," he explained.

"So, why is this not told to us?" I asked.

"Because the consciousness in the higher plane is aware of everything, but the part of it which is within the shell, it is too difficult for it to comprehend this concept, and hence, in order to give it a purpose to finish the test, the concept of heaven, hell and all things related to them are preached in the mortal realm." he said.

"Then what about God? Is he also only a concept, built on false illusions??"

"Understand this–whom you refer to as God is actually the entity that is guiding you through the test; in other words, the entity that you are a part of. People have always wanted to believe in a form of messiah–that someday some savior will come and save them, and everything will be fine after that. In fact, that is why there is so much disorientation regarding God. But if you read those religious texts of yours, you will find that most of them say that God resides in everyone. Now if you hold it in comparison to the test, it is true indeed," he replied.

"I still don't get it ... if it is only a test then why is there so much hunger, poverty, and sadness in the world? I mean, there are good things also but, what about the negative forces and negative people that are causing terrorism and causing harm to others?"

"Child, even though a coach is an excellent player, he still never plays the game. He can only guide the players. Similarly, when a shell is conjured in existence, it is very easy for it to get distracted and go on a different path. There are rules to this test, that the entity can only guide the soul but cannot interfere with mortal affairs. And these evil people that you talk about are souls that have taken the wrong path and, hence, are now trapped in the test," he said.

"So, now will you tell me what is this Sanctum and where is it?" I asked another time.

"The Sanctum, in your words, can be defined to be existing in the fifth dimension, above time. Time, here, is not linear as you have experienced in your life; instead, we can move in it, as we move in space," he replied.

"So how did I get here?" I asked.

"Your mortal body died in the presence of the soul-keeper, that is why your soul was exempted from the test and you were sent here," he said.

"You mean to say, at the hospital when I was shot, right?"

"No, at your apartment where you lived, when the blast happened," he answered.

"But after that, I woke up in a hospital ... and they said it was a miracle that I survived ... and th-then I even got shot at the hospital! That's when I died" I blabbered.

"Oh, is that what you believe? You died at your apartment but since you were in the presence of the soul-keeper, your guiding entity was able to reconjure your shell; let me explain–just like–perhaps a checkpoint in a videogame. Usually, it takes a while for a soul that is selected for the sanctum to be able to connect to its entity and be able to reconjure their previous shell," he enlightened.

"Oh, is that right? So it means I am special that I was able to do it so quickly? I blurted with a tone of arrogance in my voice.

"Yes, it could very well be, but you know there is one specific way to describe your greatness here," he said excitedly.

"And what is that?" I asked.

"Beginner's luck," he said with a smirk on his face.

"Oh ... okay," I replied with a sigh.

"You seem to know so much about me, can you then tell me why is that?" I asked, curiously.

"Yes, because we've been watching over you ever since you took possession of the soul-keeper," he replied.

"What?! So why didn't you help me before this? Even when I was shot?" I asked.

"Because, you see, we are not allowed to interfere with the worldly matters of the mortals. We can only intervene once they have arrived at the Sanctum," he motioned at the place around.

"Okay, yes ... But, wait! You still didn't answer me about my bird story, could you please explain to me what was it?" I asked.

"Oh yes yes, I'll tell", he said.

"See when you are selected for the sanctum, you have to go through a place known as the passage. There you are given a shell entirely different from your original form, in order to see whether you are fit for the sanctum. Most souls, after entering this newly given shell, tend to forget their purpose and become engrossed in that shell. The other beings that you would have met in that place are those souls," he said.

"Hmm. I also remember one hooded fellow being there," I said.

"Oh yes, that must have been Jake you had come across. That boy has a habit of playing around with souls that he has to escort to the sanctum, don't mind him!" he chuckled. “Come here, I have something special for you,” he said.

I leaned close to him and then he lightly kept his hand on my chest.

[Whooosh! Splash!!!] Before I could realize anything, I had flown about six feet in distance and had landed in the pond. I was in a complete shock and struggled to get my wholly drenched body out when I saw him coming towards me with a smile on his face.

“What was that?” I demanded.

“This was an example of gravity manipulation, and also a lesson to teach you not to bite more than what you can chew. Just because I have shared the knowledge with you doesn’t mean that you are now a great being with superhuman qualities. You are still a novice at this. Your training will begin in some time. So, go, get changed, and be there on time. You are dismissed for now,” he declared and left.

“Yes, Master” I replied.

I got myself out of the pond and then headed for my room to get changed and be ready for my training.

07

One thing that I observed during my stay there was that the masters never said "meet me tomorrow" or "today". They would only ask us to meet "after some time". I guessed that maybe it was because time had no effect on that dimension. And even the days and nights didn't have a pattern, as the sky was never devoid of light.

After having a change of clothes and taking some rest, I went into the garden. Master Sheng was already waiting for me. I smiled at him.

"Bow down and show some respect, you illiterate nincompoop!" he scowled.

"Oh, right! Yes, master," I replied nervously while bowing down to him.

"Now come with me to the pond," he said.

I followed.

He dipped his hands into the pond and then cupped them together to draw some water out. He then took his hands and parted them midway. It was so quick that, expecting a splash, I closed my eyes. After a second, when I didn't hear anything, I slowly opened them. As my vision became clear, I could see a strange transparent oval-shaped orb floating in front of me. It took a moment for me to realize that it was the water that he drew out of the pond. It was floating midair.

"Water can be one of the easiest as well as one of the most difficult elements to control. That's because it reflects the state of your inner self. The more troubled you are from inside, the more difficult it will be to control it. Now you give it a try," he said, while pushing that floating orb towards me.

At first, it seemed easy, but as soon as he left the control, it seemed as if someone had given me a 100-kilo weight in each hand, and also tied one around my neck. It just felt too heavy, and within a second, I finally heard the expected splash!

"Try it again. Did you now think that you can harness gravity that easily, you idiot? Come on, try!" he commanded.

I put my hands in the pool and cupped them to draw some water out. But as I lifted them and tried to part them and make the water stay in midair, the pressure that I felt on my body was even greater than the last time. Once again, I couldn't hold it for more than a few seconds.

[Splash!]

"Again!" he ordered.

[Splash!]

"Again!" came his voice.

[Splash!]

"Once again!" he went on.

[Splash!]

After what seemed about a hundred trials, I was completely drained. By now, I was gasping for air. My chest felt heavy as if I had just pulled a truck.

"I can't ... I can't do it!" I shouted, while panting.

"Why?" he asked.

"I-I just c-can't," I sighed.

"Give me a reason," he said.

"I just can't handle the pressure, it's too much!"

"Why can't you handle it?"

"What? I just told you I can't because it's too much for my body," I said, irritated.

"Try again!"

"I can't"

"Try again, I said"

"I really cannot"

"Why?" he asked, for the hundredth time.

Now I was getting really frustrated with the situation and his irrationality.

"I am telling you–I simply can't do it as my body is unable to handle it anymore. I've reached my limit. Why the hell can't you understand this simple point?" I yelled at him with all the energy that was left in me.

"Because, dimwit, you don't have a body to begin with!" he replied with a stern face.

"Huh? What?!", I asked, flabbergasted.

"Yes. Did you really think that your mortal shell was able to cross the mortal realm and be present in this fifth dimension with you?" he questioned.

I found the question to be rhetorical so I decided to remain quiet.

"What you now think of as your body is only an image that your soul has brought with it from the mortal realm, just like a snapshot of what you used to look like," he said.

"I still don't understand," I replied confusedly.

"When you died, your soul had an image of you, and that is what you see here in the fifth dimension. When your soul entered here, in order to give you a sense of being, it projected that image of you, similar to an astral projection. And, dimwit, since you have always lived in a shell you believed it and also brought along the limitations of it with you," he explained.

"Now try to let go of these limitations, and try again. But before that, clear your mind," he said.

His words had some effect on me. So, I slowly bent down to draw water in my hands. But this time, instead of directly trying to drop the water and then catch it midair, I thought to first try to raise it from my hands. As soon as I started to concentrate, I could feel the pressure building upon my body. Slowly and gradually it was becoming more and more difficult for me to hold the water, just like before.

"Now don't resist the force. Try to bend with it," I heard a whisper. I tried to follow it. Now instead of trying to control or rather withstand the pressure, I just let it go through me. And it seemed almost like magic that it was becoming easier. I could now balance the orb of water in the air a few inches above my palm. Although its shape was still difficult to control, but I was happy that at least I managed to get the basics of it.

"Gravity is one of nature's fundamental forces. It cannot be controlled. The reason you were not being able to hold the orb previously was because you were trying desperately to control it. You will have to understand that you can only have gravity aid you in your task, you can only be a channel to direct it, never its master. You are now dismissed. Meet me after some time," he said and then strode away.

As I was walking away from the garden, completely drenched, all these past days started coming back to me. Only a few days ago, I was this guy who was working in FedEx and had a monotonous job. Whereas now, I was practicing to manipulate gravity in the fifth dimension. A lot had happened. All those memories that I had of things that had happened to me–me being a bird and all–now seemed to be only a figment of my imagination. My thoughts had become fluid and kept intertwining the more I thought about them. I was unable to put them in chronological order. Maybe being in that place affected my perception of time. But, some questions constantly started to creep into my mind–*What was the point of all this? After learning all this, what purpose would I serve? I mean, there has to be something that I need to do after amassing all these skills and knowledge, right?* I thought of all of these things while I strolled to my room.

After a while when I had changed and was resting, I heard a soft knock on my door. I slid it open and could see a little boy with gleaming blue eyes look up at me. He barely seemed to be about the age of seven or eight. He was holding some kind of book that was heavier than his arms could handle. He gestured me to take the book. I took it from him, and then he started to walk away.

"Hey what should I do with this? And who has sent it?" I asked.

The boy, while still walking away, turned his head and in a cute, childish voice said, “I think you should read it, dimwit. [hehehe].” he giggled and ran away.

“Wait!! Wha...?” I wondered, a little confused. And suddenly, it dawned upon me that who had sent the book.

I smiled and turned around while closing the door behind me.

I sat down in my room while still keeping the book in my hand. I examined the book. The book seemed quite old. It had a red, leather cover over it, and a brown leather strap wrapped around it. I could feel some engravings beneath the leather cover but couldn’t figure out what they were. It was a thick book with roughly around 500 pages. From the outside, it seemed that all the pages had turned yellow. It had the old book smell to it.

I slowly placed the book in front of me and began untying the strap. It seemed to be a little tight at first, but after giving it a little jerk, it opened fine.

08

As I turned over to the first page, I came across a symbol I did not understand and wasn't able to comprehend what it meant. I flipped the pages over anyway. Strangely, neither did the book have a title, nor a contents' table. After a few blank pages, it just started with some text with a small heading that said, "Gravity Manipulation". I was just glad that the book was in English and not some cryptic old age language. It seemed strange though, but I decided to give it a read. The content of this chapter was some fundamentals about gravity. It described how it can be harnessed. It had one specific line– "Gravity is a force; your soul should be the channel through which it should flow, and not your body." This left me a little confused, but I was excited to read the whole thing so I kept reading and turning one page after another.

Halfway through some pages, I found a topic that read: "The Five Senses Trap"

The mortal shell has been given five senses through which it perceives its surroundings. In the shell's common tongue these are classified as–Sight, Hearing, Touch, Taste, and Smell. Each of these help the shell to survive. But shells unknowingly get too attached to these senses. They forget that the shell itself is only a container and the piece of consciousness that they carry within themselves is far greater in sensing danger from a distance. Yet, they rely on these senses for everything and, hence, fall into the trap. The five senses were not only designed to help the shell survive, but also to keep the shell attached to the mortal realm. Their ultimate motive was to keep the shell distracted and cling onto them blindly so that they forget their purpose and get distracted from the test and fall into the loop of death and life. This is known as the Five Senses Trap.

This was all making sense to me, as now I could imagine my life and how I was actually a part of this test, yet completely ignorant of all this. On reading further, there was another topic that read: "The Entity Connection"

The shells are aware of the presence of consciousness inside them (they refer to it as the soul). Some choose to ignore its presence and some choose to accept it. But undeniably these shells have an entity or, rather, a fragment of the interdimensional consciousness within them. When a shell is newly formed (birth) then the connection between the entity and the shell is the strongest. As the shell grows, the connection starts to fade. But there is always a hidden link that is present between these two—a connection that can be referred to as a bond. This bond stretches beyond the plane of existence. The consciousness can use this bond to guide the shell. Since the shell in its mortal form is unable to understand the language of the immortals, this bond converts those messages or thoughts of the being into experiences of the shell, that is, something that the shell sees or feels. The shells refer to it as Intuition. This connection is always present between the two; it only changes its state from being strong to weak. However, if a shell can focus properly, it can easily strengthen this connection, and have a communication with the higher entity."

Blue Eyes of Hope

There comes a time when the shells are able to connect with their consciousness and start to act in complete harmony with it. Their independent existence ends and becomes a part of the original thought from which they emerged. If the shell then chooses to retain its original form, then this harmony will be reflected in the form of blue rings in their eyes—also known as Rings of Hope. Having achieved this state, the shell can surpass its current physical and mental limits.

Death Sword

The Death Sword or Sword of Death is a mystic sword and has been reported to conjure itself in a random fashion throughout the mortal history. The origin of the sword is unknown, but legend has it that the sword is a lethal weapon, and if any being is killed by it, he does not die but is rather wiped from the plane of existence, or he goes through true death.

Reincarnation

There is a certain phenomenon in which the consciousness is able to reconjure any one of its older shells after its imminent death in the mortal realm. This shell is sometimes able to retain its memories and experiences from past lives as well. This process is known as Reincarnation in the mortal realm.

I was engrossed into the book, when I suddenly heard someone knock on my door. I could see the shadow of a child standing across the door. I slid the door open. It was the same boy from before who had come to give me the book.

"Master has called for you, follow me," he said impatiently.

"Ah! Okay," I replied a little bit confused and started to follow him down the hallway. He led me to the same room that I first came from.

There still was a chair kept in the middle and only master Sheng was standing in front of it with a small vial of some dark liquid in his hand. He asked me sit on the chair by pointing at it. No sooner did I sit down, than he said, "You must leave immediately. You are not safe here!"

“What?” I asked incredulously. “What are you saying? What does it even mean? What’s wrong?”

“There simply is no time to explain,” he said hurriedly.

Before I could even react or reply, he gave me a tight punch in my gut. The punch felt so heavy that it seemed to move my internals from left to right. The thrust of punch made me exhale the air from my lungs. And as soon as I looked up and tried to open my mouth to breathe and get back to my senses, he just opened the vial and jammed it in my mouth. I could feel the liquid flowing down my throat and being spilt on my cheeks as well. It was all too quick for me to act on my reflexes. And before I could wrap my mind around it, everything started to go dark–pitch black. I tried to get up and move away, but my limbs failed me. My body started feeling heavy and I thought I would be crushed under my weight. And then the darkness engulfed me as everything went silent. Everything but a faint echo–”Find your purpose...”–and it drifted away.

09

I could hear some noises at a distant. The more I concentrated on it, the more I became aware of my senses and my surroundings. I slowly opened my eyes and realized that I was in a room, on a bed, and all of this looked strangely familiar. I slowly woke up and to my surprise, it was my private room back at the hospital! The noises from the outside kept going on. I looked outside the window and it was still dark. I checked the clock; it was 2 AM. I decided to go out and see what the commotion was all about.

I still felt drowsy as I walked towards the door. As I opened my door, I could now clearly hear the words. The voice seemed of a man, shouting "Where is he? Let us know and nobody gets hurt." A woman answered while sobbing, "I have already told you. I do not know him. I cannot help you, just let me go."

As my eyes adjusted to the brightness of the corridor, I could see two men in black suits. They were both well-built and were wearing black sunglasses. This was rather queer. One of them was holding the woman by her hair and the other stood there as if looking out for his partner, they both were holding a gun in their hands ... and looked like hench—-

Wait a minute!

A sudden realization of *déjà vu* came rushing back to me. This exact same scene had happened with me even before. While thinking, unconsciously, I moved my door aside and a creaking sound came from it. I looked up for confirmation of the previously happened incident and to my horror, I could see that the other guy nudged his partner. The partner looked at me and then they started walking towards me. In a matter of seconds, I was facing two huge men. *What should I do?* I thought to myself.

"Are you Jayden Smith?" asked one of them. And like a stupid guy, I replied, "Yes, I am," and then gulped nervously.

Before I could say or do anything, they forcibly covered my mouth with their hand and one guy pressed his gun against my chest. My mind was flooded with thoughts, my heart was racing. But at that moment, something happened. As my body was pumped with adrenaline, everything started to slow down. I could see the guy's finger slowly gripping the trigger of the gun. I could also feel a surge of energy growing inside me, and it made me feel stronger. I made up my mind; *not this time*. And before the guy could press the trigger, I kicked him in his chest with all the might I had in me. In a fraction of a second, I could see him flying through the air and crashing in the wall in front. The other guy suddenly pointed his gun towards me, but to his surprise, he received a side-kick in his chest, which sent him flying 3 feet in the air towards the other wall against which he crashed and fell.

Oh, my fucking god! I have superpowers! I thought in that hyperactive and excited state of mine. The guy who was hit by the side-kick lay completely still. While the guy in front of me had started to come back to his senses. My excitement was now coming down and I started to become more aware of my surroundings. As I calmed down, I could see the terrified faces of the people who were present in the corridor. I sensed that it wouldn't be wise to stay there anymore. So, without wasting any more time, I rushed into my room, grabbed whatever I could, stuffed them in a bag, and started to leave in a hurry. When I came outside of my room, I could still see the big guy's failed attempts at getting himself up from the ground, while the other guy seemed to be still passed out. As I went by the unconscious guy, I could see a small card lying near him. I took it without thinking anything. And then began walking as fast as I could, dodging the security guards and some hospital staff who were heading towards the area of action. Soon, in a few minutes, I was at a safe distance from the hospital complex.

Walking alone on the pavement, my mind was exploding with thoughts. *What did I just do now? And how the hell did I end up at the same place and same situation again? And above all–why were those guys looking for me? Who were they?* At present, I had nowhere to go, and now knowing that these people were after me, I had to make sure that no one gets in danger because of me. While constantly filtering my thoughts about where to spend the night, I suddenly remembered something. Judging from the hospital's location and the direction I was walking in, I had a memory of an abandoned factory near the outskirts of the city. When we were younger, I and my friends had found the place which had an underground hidden room, secluded in one corner of the factory. We had conveniently turned it into our hideout, and called it "The Cave". Hoping that no one else had found it after we had left, it would be a good place to hide right now. So, I quickened my steps and headed towards the factory. After walking quite a distance, I finally reached the factory's fence. Now, by memory, I started to look for the spot in the fence wire from where we used to sneak in. I was surprised to see how I somehow managed to find it and then finally made my way inside. The place looked exactly how we had left it–ruined but intact. I found the door and let myself in. Since the door was the only way out and it didn't seem to be opened by anyone in a long while, it gave me a sense of security while entering it. As I entered the room and closed the door slowly behind me, I instinctively went for the switchboard to turn on the lights. [CLICK!] Nothing happened. [CLICK! CLICK! CLICK!] Still no luck. I guessed maybe they had cut the power of that place. While feeling the wall, I bent down and suddenly touched a solid object. It instantly filled me with relief. It was a cylindrical shaped object with an oval top. I picked it up and started to feel for a button and, in a moment or two, I found it. I pressed it with a click and suddenly there was light in the room. I could see the dust-covered sofa that we had brought from a junkyard and a slab of wood placed over four bricks, serving as a makeshift table. I carefully kept the object on the table and dusted the sofa with my bag. As I sat, I could see the walls covered with a poster that was almost peeling off the wall. A smile came across my face. This place was dusty and dingy but for some strange reason, it felt like home.

10

Next morning, I woke up to a dingy smell of a closed room, with an occasional swirl of dust in the air as I adjusted my body on the sofa. As I opened my eyes, I could see the light piercing through the sides of the doorway. I switched the lamp on to fill the room with light. I had a pack of chips and some bread, that I had found in my bag, for breakfast. And now my thoughts started to fall in an alignment. So, I took some of the leftover utilities–remains from my old gang–and set up a whiteboard to analyze the crazy ongoing situation.

First of all, I had to find out why I was being followed by those guys. All of a sudden, I remembered the card that I had taken from that guy from my encounter. I pulled it out and I could see a visiting card, with just a symbol in front of the card, which looked like a blue flower designed with only blue parallel lines. And at the back of the card, I could see only a name printed that said "KYLAR INDUSTRIES". Now, this seemed rather odd to me. Because Kylar Industries was a mammoth of an organization. They had their hands into everything– be it the bank, the infrastructure or the transport.

What could they possibly want from a guy like me? The more I thought about it, the further confused I got. Because to me, it absolutely made no sense. Just as I was deep into my thoughts, I could hear some distant noises which seemed to echo in the room and was coming nearer. I quickly got out to see where that noise was coming from. I climbed up one of the processing-tower in the factory to get a bird's eye view.

To my horror and surprise, I could see a trail of cars and some military vehicles coming straight towards the factory and they all had Kylar industries logo on them. I was panicking. I quickly climbed down, got my stuff and was moving towards the back of the factory. There was a huge water-tank tower at the back; that was where we had our secret exit right next to it.

My breathing was quickly escalating, I could hear the screech of the tires as they came to a frantic stop. I could hear the doors closing and a number of footsteps crawling all over the place. I made a run for it. I could hear the footsteps getting closer. I was now sweating profusely. Finally, I could see the gate and I was running frantically towards it. The footsteps were getting closer and closer.

"STOPPP!" I heard a voice shout followed by the sound of load-click of a gun from behind. My heart suddenly dropped a beat, and everything came to halt. I slowly turned around my head to see who it was. I could see a heavily built guy in a military dress. He was pointing his machine gun at me and was slowly approaching me. The footsteps had now turned into that of a dozen people and, in a matter of seconds, I was completely surrounded from all the sides, with guns pointing at me from every direction.

"ON YOUR KNEES! Arms behind your back!" the guy yelled from behind.

Without further ado, I obeyed, asking no questions and got on my knees. He quickly came towards me and pointed his machine gun dead against the back of my head. I closed my eyes with the hopes of the worst possible outcome.

"You think you can run out on us, huh? What a punk!" he said smugly, pressing the gun harder against my head. My eyes were still closed; I did not know what to do or say; my throat felt heavy and I couldn't speak. But, something started to rise inside me. I could now remember the happenings of the day before. And I could feel the powerful energy surge through me, growing stronger inside me. I could feel the power starting to flow into my veins. I could feel it slowly growing from my stomach towards my limbs. It honestly felt good as this streak passed in my muscles. And as it ran up my spines, I was slowly becoming full of it.

"You wanna fight, punk? You shithead! Who do you think you are? The man said. "You wanna fight, eh? Come on then! Get Up! What's the matter? Punk!" he was screaming at me.

For some reason, at that point I've had enough of this. This confusion, this chaos, this uncertainty.

So, I opened my eyes.

"As a matter of fact, I do," I replied.

And before he could react, I reached for the tip of the gun and bent it like a plastic tube in the shape of a horizontal-U. Next, I quickly stood up eye to eye, facing him and delivered a huge double punch in his stomach which sent him flying backwards on two of his comrades.

I am not going to run away this time, I am going to show these assholes they messed with the wrong guy. And I charged at them. I was too fast for them to react. I took the guy standing right behind me by his arms and hit him with my knee. [CRACKK!] and then a knockout punch was enough for him to fall on the floor. The other guys immediately charged at me all at once. I could see this in slow motion now. Everything was clear to me—I could see their muscles flinch as they tightened their wrists to form a punch. I could see their cheeks tighten as they were charging towards me. I was all pumped up and full-on ready to take them on.

I dodged the first guy's punch, then ducked under him, giving him the upper fist cut which sent him flying away. Other two guys came at me from the front. The guy behind me received a double punch while another got a back kick. And now, I was facing five people at once. I redirected the punch of the first guy to hit the third guy, stopped the second guy's kick with my fist and the fourth guy's kick with my kick. I applied thrust upon these two with all my might and they went down with a loud thud. The fifth guy and I were now standing face to face. He threw me a punch which I immediately blocked. Then a kick which almost hit my face and I had to catch it with both my hands. Now It was my turn. I turned his feet with all my strength, and caused the guy to roll midair, and then, while still holding his feet, took my hand and smacked him on the floor like we give a smackdown to a rolled carpet. [THUD!] This one was surely done for the day. I raised and cracked my knuckles. I could see the last two guys who were standing at a distance; they were shaking. I could see the sweat pouring down their forehead, the nervousness and fear in their eyes, and the chill that ran down their spine, travelling rapidly through their bodies, making them helpless and immobile. I ran towards them in order to finish what was started. I grabbed the guy by the collar and lifted him in the air.

[SWOOSH! KACHINGGGGG!] I felt something on my back. [CRACK! CRACK! BUZZZ!] The last thing I heard was a grunt and then everything suddenly was wrapped in darkness.

11

[BEEP! SHOOSH! BEEP! SHOOSH! BEEP!]

Peculiar sounds reverberated in my ears. As I tried to open my eyes, it was instantly flooded with a bright white light so I had to shut it. I couldn't smell anything; the air seemed clean and fresh. After waiting for some time, I slowly tried to open my eyes. I could see a white substance all over me and my feet were visible at the end. I looked to my right to see a machine from where the beeping sounds were coming. And to my left, there was a machine that had some sort of pump that was making the swishing kind of Sound. Getting back to consciousness seemed to be quite a hectic task at that moment, forget about moving. I was, in fact, struggling even to keep my eyes open and see things clearly. My head was swirling in a frenzy. It seemed as if I was in a state of constant motion and I couldn't stop myself.

After a failed attempt, my eyes fell like a curtain on a stage. Some moments later, something broke my slumber and started echoing in my ears. [tip tap tip tap tip] It got louder and louder till I came back to my senses and forcefully opened my eyes. This time the frenzy in my head seemed to be reduced and things in front of me were easier to focus on.

[TIP TAP TIP TAP]

The sounds came from my left and stopped in front of me, a grey, lucid image appeared right before me, which upon looking intently, turned out to be a person in a grey suit. His hair was silver and well combed. He was clean-shaven and had a lot of wrinkles on his face. His cheeks were like valleys of the Himalayas and he wore frameless glasses which magnified his zombie-like eyes. He stood with his arms crossed and as stiff as a dead body. After a moment of silence, he said, "Hi, Mr Smith, I hope you are feeling better this morning."

Feeling better?! What nonsense is this? I asked myself, but couldn't utter a word.

"My name is Samuel Kylar, I am the head of Kylar Industries. It's a pleasure to meet you," he said with those dry, autumn-leaf-like lips of his.

"Huh?" I scowled.

"You are a difficult person to find now, aren't you, Mr Smith? But thank god, we just keep a tab on each of our company's belongings, just to be safe, you know," he said with a smirk.

And suddenly, it struck me. I knew now exactly how they had tracked me down at the factory. I tried to slowly move my body but failed to do so. I tried again but with no significant results.

"Well, well, Mr Smith, these attempts of yours in order to move–let me inform you–they won't work. From your previous interaction with our employees, we are absolutely clear that you are not trustworthy with your arms and legs. So, we had to sedate you. But you know, you became a very good test subject for our prototype electric clutches though," he said in a disturbingly calm voice.

"Why are ... you ... uggh ... w-why do you ... want m-me?" I struggled to blurt in my current state.

"What did you say? Want you? Hahaha! NO, no, we certainly don't want you. You understand, Mr Smith, this company is like my child. And just like any other parent, I am also only trying to protect my baby from harm, that you might bring upon her," he said.

"What? ... I ... harm?" I whimpered.

"Oh! I know that you have nothing to do with this, but let me clear it out for you," he continued. "You remember the bomb blast that you survived? Well, let's just say it was not a blast, rather, a nanite leakage accident. Now these babies of mine were made to annihilate everything in their path, and they were very good at it too, but you know since we lost control of them, we had to do an EMP burst in the nearby areas to deactivate them, all my poor children had to be turned into black dust. Now, this news of a bomb explosion which radiated an excess amount of heat that wiped everyone and everything in its path was well circulated and acknowledged by all, right? You were supposed to be dead, Mr. Smith. In fact, we went on to push the news of your death out there and made sure that you never woke up. Do you have any idea how much effort it took? But you know, this miraculous recovery of yours—after the blast—and that too without a trace of radiation, had started to raise some eyebrows. Alas! You just cannot trust other people for your work these days. So, I decided to take matters in my own hands—and see—here we are!" he exclaimed.

"You call killing thousands … an accident?" I was slowly regaining my speaking ability.

"Oh, of course! Yes, those people just happened to be in the wrong place at the wrong time, that's all," he shrugged, smiling.

My rising temper had reached its peak. With whatever strength that was left in me, I threw myself at him. [SWOOSH!! CLANK!] I stopped abruptly midway as my arms were restrained by metal chains that held me back while my face was an inch away from his. I was filled with rage and my hot breath was now touching his skin and my eyes were locked into his.

He took a step back and wiped his face, and said "Now, now, don't be angry, Mr Smith! I assure you in sometime everything will be fine," he then snapped his fingers and six muscular men came rushing in and held me by the chains and secured me in my bed.

He then just smirked and turned away, walking outside the room, signaling a doctor who was standing at the door. The doctor entered the room with a syringe in his hand.

"NO!! Let me go!!" I was struggling to get free from the clasps of the men. The doctor was coming closer.

"Hold him still!" the doctor screamed.

At this moment, my mind was filled with a multitude of thoughts. I was angry and disgusted at Kylar's arrogance and cruelty. My medication or whatever it was that they gave me was wearing off. I was not going to let him escape so easily. But my first priority was to escape from this place and survive first. The Doctor was now grabbing my arm as well and was about to inject me. I started to channel my energy and whatever was left in me, in my arm. He went ahead and thrusted the syringe in my arm. [SWOOOSH! CLUNK! CLINK!] He stood startled as the blue liquid spilt in each direction.

This was my chance. I could feel like myself again. I gave a huge jerk to both my arms. The guards backed off a bit. And I was able to break the chains that were holding me. Now I was standing free on my bed. The energy surge was now back in me. I could see a blue aura around my body. The guards now pounched on me I jumped to avoid them. One of them caught my leg and pulled me down.

[THRASH!] I fell on the floor. I quickly got up and was now facing 6 huge men. I was getting more pumped up by the action. I realized that I could see their eye lids close in slow motion. And I was able to see the tracjectory that their punches would follow. So, I quickly went head on into them. Punched the first guy from the left, that sent him flying backwards. Barely dodged the three incoming punches from the guys and ducked down to block a kick from the fourth guy in mid air. I then gathered all my might and while holding the guy's leg made him crash into the other three.

[SMASH!!]

Now there was one more to go. He backed off a bit, but then was charging towards me. I just quickly moved from his path and grabbed a small medical steel tray and hit it as hard as I could against his face.

[CLANK! TUNG! SMASH!]

As I eyed the mess of the people and things lying around with satisfaction, I quickly headed for the door.

I went through the door and found myself in a circular lobby. From a rough estimate, it seemed like I was on the fifth floor. I frantically started looking for any sign of Kylar. I saw him moving towards a door on the opposite side of the floor into a room. I followed him quietly. My mind was whirling with the cries of the thousands of innocents who had to die that fateful night. I followed him into the room slowly, closing the door behind me.

12

The room was dimly lit and had a red carpet on the floor. The room's walls were covered with a lime green wallpaper. There was a work desk on one side of the room. Behind it, there were two huge French windows, which were also covered with red drapes. There was no sign of light piercing through them, so I guessed it must be night already. In the other corner of the room, there was a fireplace which was casting a yellow tinge to its side and most of it was blocked by what seemed like a green velvet chair. Everything was quiet as the dead, except the crackling woods in the fireplace. There was no sign of anyone in the room. I was surprised. *But I just saw him get in here!* I told myself. I decided to look into the room for anything that could lead me to him. I was frantically searching for any clues that might lead me to him.

I looked under the desk, behind the chair, even drew the drapes, but nothing exceptional—except the moonlight that poured in from the night sky. As I bent down to see beneath the chair, something caught my attention.

[PHOOOOOOH!]

There was a faint sound of wind gushing into the place. I stood at fixed, and closed my eyes, trying hard to focus on the sound. It took me a while to figure out, but I pinpointed it to be coming from one side of the fireplace. I walked up to it and put my ear intently against it in the hope of accurately locating the sound. About an inch upwards from the right bottom corner of the fireplace, I found out that there was a crack from which the air was blowing in. I tapped on the fireplace boundary, the mantlepiece, and it seemed that it was hollow from inside. So, I jabbed my fingers and tried to pull. After a while, the fireplace seemed to move, thereby, revealing a stairway leading downwards.

I carefully started going downstairs. After a few more steps, when I was about to reach the end, I could hear some muffled noises of two people talking. From where I was, I could make out that it was a man and a woman talking. I carefully reached the end and hid behind a wall near the entry to a hall-like room. I peeked a few times, and could only see a huge hall-like structure with grey pillars supporting the huge ceiling. Kylar was standing at the center with his back facing towards the gate. And a woman was standing beside him, holding a tray with what looked like a teacup on it.

He then took the cup from the tray, the lady suddenly looked in the direction where I was hiding. I quickly hid back in my position. "This is still cold," I heard him say.

"I ... I am sorry, Mr Kylar," the lady fumbled nervously.

"No, no, child, don't be sorry. I forgive you," He replied in his eerie voice.

"Re-Really Mr Kyla—-aaaAAAGGHH!!"

[SMASHHH!]

I quickly turned to see what was the matter, and to my horror, the lady was floating midair as Kylar grabbed her by her throat and raised her upwards.

[CRACK!]

She fell with a soft thud.

I was breathing heavily. I was shocked to see such a monster that Kylar actually was.

"Hello, Mr Smith!" a voice said from behind me.

I quickly turned around to see Kylar standing right there. Before I could even react, I could see his hands tighten around my throat and then I was hurled to the center of the hall. I landed with a thud, right next to the girl. I tried to get up but again felt a hand on me, which this time sent me flying straight into the wall in front of me.

[CRASH! THUD!]

"Aaagghh!" I groaned in pain as I rolled over my back. I had no clue what was happening. But I knew I was not here to go down without a fight. So, I gathered all my strength and got up and walked back to the center of the room.

There was no sign of Kylar. I looked in every direction but I couldn't see him.

Suddenly, I sensed someone behind my back, I quickly rolled forward barely dodging his attack.

"Now, now, Mr Smith, don't you go away," he said while standing.

I was already pissed off and now I could feel the anger gurgling within me. He charged at me. But this time I was prepared. I caught his punch with one hand and his throat with another, and instantly, picked him up and thrashed him onto the floor.

[SMASHH!]

I had lost my cool now. Every vein in my body was pumped, my pulse was throbbing. I climbed up on him and started landing punches in a frenzy on his face.

[BASH! BOOM! BASH!]

One after the other, I was throwing him fists and punches, pouring all my stress into it. All this confusion, anxiety and frustration that were haunting my mind had finally found a vent to be channeled out. I kept thrashing him, left and right, with all the strength that I had left. After a point, he just laid there like a bag of sand.

After my anger had subsided, I got up and turned to walk away.

"AAHHH!!" came from behind me. I stopped to turn around.

Kylar was writhing on the ground and was now struggling to get up. I stood there dumbstruck. And right in front of my eyes, he got up. The sight was ghastly and horrific. His face was disfigured completely, his lips had become swollen and had become dark blue in color. His eyes were violet and he couldn't even open them. There was a clear dent in his skull, his cheeks had both sunken in his jaws, and his face was bloody all over with gashes and bruises.

"YOU!!!" he bellowed, pointing his finger at me. "SCOUNDREL!" he screamed at the top of his voice.

[CRACK!!! CRACK!!! CRACK!!]

His body jolted with each sound.

"I am going to FINISH YOU!" he threatened, grumbling in a voice deep enough like a possessed spirit we have only seen in horror movies. His body was changing rapidly–sharp teeth began to protrude from his mouth, going out of proportion and tearing his lips apart; his eyes were becoming a black ocean; his hand and legs were growing in size and a black fur covered them; his back had become hunched and his suit's cloth which had begun to tear in places, revealed sharp bone-like structures rising from within.

In a moment or so, I was facing a towering beast in front of me. It had a humanoid appearance but was more like a mix of giant gorilla and gargoyle.

"You think you can defy us?!" he asked in his demonic voice.

[SLIKK]

He pulled out one of the sharp structures from his back, and it looked like a bone sword.

"I am going to show you, rascal, what your place really is", he said, while slowly charging towards me.

"We, the noble race of Netvor, have ruled this realm from the beginning of time, and you mortal think that you can defy us?!" he screamed.

[SMASH!]

I barely dodged his attack.

"WE WILL WIPE YOUR SPECIES OUT OF EXISTENCE!" he was getting infuriated.

[SMASHHH!]

Another attack I somehow dodged but my arm got a slicing cut and blood was oozing out now. I was desperate to find a way out as by each attack I was being cornered and the door was past the monster Kylar. He raised his sword again. I tried to move further back but the wall stopped me. I was finally cornered with nowhere to go.

[SWOOSH!]

He swung down his sword as I raised my arms to defend.

[SHING! CLANK!]

I was expecting some kind of blow or damage but nothing happened. I moved my arms to see that Kylar's sword was stuck midair, and an object was blocking it. It looked like a small horizontal silvery object. It also had a translucent orb-like structure at one end.

As I slowly stood up, holding my blood-soaked arm, I knew exactly what it was. The object thrust onto his sword and he flung backwards. I reached out to hold it. It flew in my hand and I remembered its silvery scales when I had first touched it. On touching it once again, it started to morph into something. A sword-like object suddenly began to reveal itself and a small part of silver substance slid out into my arms and formed a ring-like sheath around the wounded part.

In a matter of seconds, I was holding a silver sword with a dragon as its gilt. The wave of energy surged back to me, reviving every fiber of my body with power. I could see the eyes of the dragon glow with a blue hue. As I walked, I could see my reflection in the sword. My eyes had a blue ring around them.

I now was standing in front of Kylar. And now, for some reason, I simply wasn't panicking anymore. I was ready to face him.

He charged at me. [CLANK!]

We were both in a lockdown.

[SWOOSH! BAM! THUD!!!] I fell and tried to get up immediately again.

[CHINGGGG!!! CLANK!]

He was thrusting with all his might; I was barely able to block him. Facing him head-on didn't seem like a good idea.

[SMACK!! SWOOSH!!! BAM!!]

He fell backwards from my kick. The Dragon sword felt unreal as if it was somehow now a part of me. I had to think of something–and soon–because Kylar didn't seem to be in a mood to give in.

[CLINK! CLANK!]

There was another clash and we both were forced backwards.

[CLANK! SWOOSH!]

Dodging his attacks was becoming more and more difficult. He charged at me, and I ran towards him. The moment he was about to strike, I dropped my sword and slid from beneath him. I quickly stood up behind him, the sword was again in my arms.

An idea struck me.

I gripped the sword tightly; the wave of energy from me was now flowing through the sword. I could see the dragon eyes glowing brighter and a blue aura was now emanating around the blade of the sword.

He was again coming at me. I ran towards him, he raised his sword, I threw my sword at him, he dodged. I was now facing him, weaponless. He swung his sword hard, downwards at me. It took everything in me to catch his arms and block the attack. And as soon as I raised my eyes—-

[SWOOSSHHH! SLINK!]

"AGGHHH...!!! HOW D-DID Y-YOU?!" he groaned, as black fluid filled his mouth and was now overflowing with it. He stepped backwards and fell on his knees. There was a sword buried in his back which pierced through his chest.

"UGHH–You g-got m-me Mr S-Smith..." he said while coughing out the black fluid.

"But–you will never win! WE WILL DESTROY YOU MORTALS SOON!" he added.

I said nothing. I just went behind him, held my sword, and with a clean slit, put an end to his suffering.

While walking out of the place, I knew now what I had to do. The words of Master Sheng were ringing in my ears. I had found my purpose. I have to stop the Netvors from achieving their objective.

In life, we usually don't get we want, rather, we get what we need. Now I realized that Jayden Smith had died in that explosion. My old life was already over and a new destiny awaited me. I had found my path—like all other shells, I too now had a test to go through; only the syllabus for me was different now.

My fight was against the forces of darkness. And whatever happened next, one thing was for sure—

This was only the beginning, and I still had a long way to go.

Only I stood now between the mortals and the Netvors. And I was going to make sure that Netvors lost.

Why?

Because...

I now am SHADE, that would be protecting the mortal's world.